Renée Marie of France

BY MAYA ANGELOU

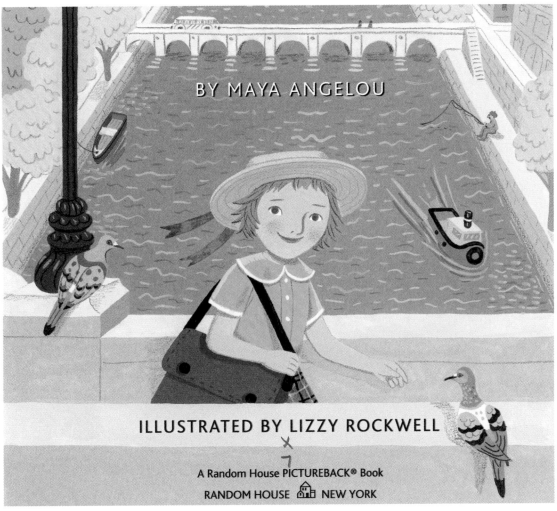

ILLUSTRATED BY LIZZY ROCKWELL

A Random House PICTUREBACK® Book

RANDOM HOUSE 🏠 NEW YORK

Text copyright © 2004 by Maya Angelou. Illustrations copyright © 2004 by Lizzy Rockwell. All rights reserved under International and Pan-American Copyright Conventions. Published in the United States by Random House Children's Books, a division of Random House, Inc., New York, and simultaneously in Canada by Random House of Canada Limited, Toronto.
www.randomhouse.com/kids
Library of Congress Cataloging-in-Publication Data
Angelou, Maya. Renée Marie of France / by Maya Angelou ; illustrated by Lizzy Rockwell. — 1st ed.   p.   cm. — (Random House pictureback)
SUMMARY: In Paris, France, Renée Marie, who is teased for being tall, goes on a school field trip to the Eiffel Tower, where she faces her fear of heights.
ISBN 0-375-82834-6 (trade) — ISBN 0-375-92834-0 (lib. bdg.)
[1. Courage—Fiction. 2. Phobias—Fiction. 3. Size—Fiction. 4. Eiffel Tower (Paris, France)—Fiction. 5. School field trips—Fiction. 6. Paris (France)—Fiction. 7. France—Fiction.] I. Rockwell, Lizzy, ill. II. Title.
PZ7.A5833Re 2004 [E]—dc22 2003021105
Printed in the United States of America   First Edition   10 9 8 7 6 5 4 3 2 1
PICTUREBACK, RANDOM HOUSE, and the Random House colophon are registered trademarks of Random House, Inc.

MAIN

When I was a little girl,

I looked around at my world.

It was small, so was I.

Then my world began to grow

With each child I came to know.

Now I try,

Now I dare

To make a new friend

Everywhere.

Let me tell you about my friend Renée Marie. She is a French girl who lives in Paris. She is *very* tall for her age. Once she shared a story with me about a special day and something else that is very tall! And now I will share it with *you*. . . .

Renée Marie went to St. Catherine's School for Girls, where the students wore smart green uniforms with white piping around the wide collars and straw hats with a dark green ribbon around the crown.

Renée Marie hated the hats. When she wore hers on top of her head, according to the rules, it made her look even taller. So she would push the hat to the back of her head.

On the way to school, she glimpsed herself in a store window. Inside the store, the shopkeeper whispered to a clerk, "She looks like an angel!"

One day Renée Marie was walking with her classmates along the lovely river Seine, which flows through the heart of Paris. They were on a class trip to the Eiffel Tower.

Everyone said that Paris was one of the most beautiful cities in the world. Renée Marie thought so, too, but of course, she had never been anywhere else, except once to visit her mean cousins in the south. She never wanted to go there again.

There were three cousins, all girls. They had laughed at her because she was so tall. Renée Marie had told her cousins that if they were lucky, they would someday grow as tall as she. They had hooted and giggled, saying, "Never, never!"

But Renée Marie didn't care what her cousins, or anyone, said. . . . She had a secret. She was studying English so that when she grew up, she could go to Hollywood and become a movie star. Movie stars are *very* tall.

The class reached the base of the Eiffel Tower, once the tallest building in the world! Renée Marie saw another group of students, all boys, waiting to go up the elevator, too. They looked a little older, and one of them was as tall as Renée Marie. He smiled at her.

"We must take the elevator to the observation level," said Madame Martine. "And we will be joined by Monsieur Belle's class." The girls giggled and whispered, but not Renée Marie. In truth, she had another secret. She was very scared of high places.

"Mesdemoiselles, follow me and stay together," said Madame Martine. The other girls trailed after Madame Martine, but Renée Marie hung back shyly, looking at souvenirs. The tall boy walked over to her.

"My name is Jacques. *Comment t'appeles-tu?*" he asked with a wide smile. "What is your name?"

She studied the trinkets and said, "Renée Marie."

"Aren't you coming?" he asked. "The elevator ride to the top will be fun."

"No, thank you. I'll stay down here," Renée Marie replied. "I can see the Tower from here." She turned to look at the young boy. Jacques had sparkly brown eyes, and he wore a pin from a riding academy on his lapel.

"It won't be the same," said Jacques. "Do come. The view must be amazing."

"So, you ride horses?" Renée Marie asked suddenly, pointing to Jacques' lapel pin.

"Yes, I take lessons," Jacques explained. "I used to be afraid of horses, but I made myself ride in spite of my fear. I won this pin in a competition. Do you ride?" Jacques asked hopefully.

"No. But I'm not afraid or anything. I would *love* to learn to ride horses," said Renée Marie. "But, Jacques? May I tell you a secret?" she whispered. "I *am* afraid of going up to the top. High places scare me!" she said, gesturing to the looming Tower above them.

"Just think of me and the horses," Jacques whispered back. "If I could do it, so can you." He held out his hand, and Renée Marie took it.

She held his hand all the way to the top. When they got out onto the observation deck, the wind was blowing hard. The other girls stood with Madame Martine, jabbering as they pointed out the great buildings and parks of Paris. The sky was blue, with puffs of cloud passing overhead. But Renée Marie's eyes were closed tight! Her heart was beating very hard in her chest.

Renée Marie took a deep breath and opened her eyes.
Together she and Jacques walked slowly to where the steel
wire netting made everything feel safer. She looked out at
the amazing view of Notre Dame and the broad avenues and
parks and the river flowing like a ribbon below.

"You see?" said Jacques. "You'll never be scared again—at least not in the same way. You are brave to have faced your fear." His words bloomed in Renée Marie's chest. She *did* feel stronger! She stood tall, and they joined her classmates to listen as Madame Martine told the history of the Tower.

The next day at school, Madame Martine asked the children to write stories about themselves and their adventure at the Eiffel Tower. Renée Marie wrote about being taller than everyone else and about Jacques and how she had "ridden the horse" in spite of her fear.

She ended her story with the wish that all who heard it would be inspired to write their own story about themselves. Oh, and most importantly, Renée Marie wants to know, "How tall are you?"

DAMAGE NOTED